# Prom Date

PRAISE FOR *STORYSHARES*

"One of the brightest innovators and game-changers in the education industry."
– Forbes

"Your success in applying research-validated practices to promote literacy serves as a valuable model for other organizations seeking to create evidence-based literacy programs."

- Library of Congress

"We need powerful social and educational innovation, and Storyshares is breaking new ground. The organization addresses critical problems facing our students and teachers. I am excited about the strategies it brings to the collective work of making sure every student has an equal chance in life."
– Teach For America

"Around the world, this is one of the up-and-coming trailblazers changing the landscape of literacy and education."
- International Literacy Association

"It's the perfect idea. There's really nothing like this. I mean wow, this will be a wonderful experience for young people."    - Andrea Davis Pinkney, Executive Director, Scholastic

"Reading for meaning opens opportunities for a lifetime of learning. Providing emerging readers with engaging texts that are designed to offer both challenges and support for each individual will improve their lives for years to come. Storyshares is a wonderful start."
- David Rose, Co-founder of CAST & UDL

# Prom Date

## Craig Merrow

STORYSHARES

Story Share, Inc.
New York. Boston. Philadelphia.

Published in the United States by Story Share, Inc.

Storyshares
Story Share, Inc.
24 N. Bryn Mawr Avenue #340
Bryn Mawr, PA 19010-3304
www.storyshares.org

*Inspiring reading with a new kind of book.*

**Interest Level:** High School
**Grade Level Equivalent:** 3.1

9781642611748

Book design by Storyshares

Printed in the United States of America

Storyshares Presents

# 1

"Twenty bucks says you can't get a prom date!" exclaimed Omar.

"Oh yeah? I'll show you!" hollered Davy over the din of students heading to class. "I can get a prom date JUST LIKE THAT!" he concluded with a snap of his fingers as he continued up the hall to his next class. Then he turned to Joshua and Karen. "That stupid Omar thinks he's going to make an easy twenty bucks off me."

Joshua thought for a moment. "So you're going to be earning this one?"

Davy scoffed at the idea. "No way! I'm sure there are lots of girls who would go to the prom with me. Watch. Hey, Karen, wanna go to the prom with me?"

"No."

Joshua shook his head. "Strike one."

"Yeah, well, she was already taken," added Davy. "You just watch! I WILL get a prom date!"

* * *

"So how did it go today?" asked Karen as she pulled her hair into a ponytail.

"Well..." said Davy, pausing as they came to a red light.

"Well?" asked Joshua.

"Well what?" asked Davy as they rumbled to a stop.

"Well, who did you ask to go to the prom?" countered Joshua.

Davy thought for a moment. "Well, so far I've asked Ellie, Amity, Michelle, Janelle, Brianna, and a few others."

"Any takers?" asked Karen.

"Yeah, all of them."

Joshua was impressed.

"You mean all of them want to go to the prom with you?"

"No, I mean they were already taken," replied Davy as he pulled away from the light.

"How many were a few others?" quizzed Karen.

"Dunno, I didn't keep score."

"I did," said Joshua. "So far you've asked thirty-seven."

"THIRTY SEVEN?" exclaimed Davy. "No way!"

"And that's not counting the classes that I don't have with him," explained Joshua to Karen. "So my figures are probably a little off."

"Help me out here, Buckwheat!" scorned Davy. "I've got twenty bucks riding on this! I WILL get a prom date!"

# 2

Karen and Joshua were eating lunch together in the school cafeteria the next day, discussing Davy's odds of getting a prom date.

"Did Davy ask anyone in your class today?" asked Joshua.

"Yeah, he asked Merriweather and Haley. Merriweather turned him down flat, and Haley said she would report him to the principal if he ever threatened her like that again."

Joshua shook his head. "Well, that ups the figure to about forty-one. He's running out of girls to ask..." trailing off when he noticed that Karen was studying her milk carton. Joshua leaned over a bit and asked, "What are you looking at?"

"I think he's starting to get desperate."

"What makes you think that?"

Karen held up her milk carton so Joshua could see it.

"Need a prom date? Call Davy Odell," he read aloud.

"How do you suppose he got his picture on a milk carton?" she asked.

* * *

"What happened to your car?" asked Karen.

Davy climbed over the windowsill. "Oh, I cut the roof off in shop class today. Women love convertibles. And I welded the doors shut, too. These four-door barges get a little flimsy when you cut half the structure away."

Joshua tossed his backpack into the car and gave Karen a boost over the door sill. "Did you have any luck today?" she asked.

"Not yet," replied Davy as he started the car.

"So who did you ask today?" asked Joshua.

"Well, I took a crack at Tory, but she turned me down."

"Why would you ask her? She's a lesbian," said Karen.

Davy shrugged. "I know, but I thought maybe she'd switch sides for a good cause."

"I think you're getting a little desperate," chided Joshua.

"Says you!" exclaimed Davy. "In fact, I'm just getting warmed up!"

"For what? The big payoff to Omar?" asked Karen.

Davy scoffed at the idea. "Very funny! Remember, I WILL get a prom date!"

# Prom Date

# 3

Davy and Joshua stopped by Karen's house later that evening, with Davy grumbling that he would get a prom date no matter what. Then he looked up through the ceiling register.

"Hey, Kara!"

Kara peered down through the grate at Davy. "What do YOU want?"

"Wanna go to the prom?"

Kara suddenly livened up. "Sure! I'd love to go!"

Davy turned to Karen. "See? I TOLD you I would get a prom date."

"With YOU? What kind of prom date is THAT?" shouted Kara.

"What?" Davy shouted back. "What's wrong with going to the prom with me?"

"Where do I begin?" Kara scoffed back at him.

"Oh yeah? Give me just ONE good reason why you won't go to the prom with me."

"Jimmy Ferguson."

Davy was silent for a moment. "Jimmy Ferguson? JIMMY FERGUSON? Why would you go to the prom with HIM?"

"Because he asked me first, so there!" And with that, Kara slapped the shutters closed in the register, ending the conversation.

Just then Karen's father, Carl, entered the room. "What are you making so much racket about?"

Davy plunked himself into a chair. "Oh, Kara won't go to the prom with me. What kind of daughter are you raising up there?"

"A very smart one," came the sarcastic reply. "Besides, what makes you think that I would let YOU take my daughter to the prom?"

"Because I'm huggable, loveable, and adorable?"

Carl greeted this with a hard stare, so Davy tried a different tactic.

"Ok, how about because I'm like the son you never had?"

"That's right, you ARE like the son I never had, and never want, either!"

Just then Annie, Karen's mother, entered the room, to whom Davy complained, "Mom, Dad doesn't want me!"

Annie looked at him in surprise. "What?"

"Davy thinks he's the son that Dad never had," explained Karen.

"Maybe that's why I have the mailman's eyes," quipped Davy to Joshua.

"You do NOT have the mailman's eyes!" exclaimed Carl. "I know that for a fact because I've raised you like...like..." he trailed off. He looked at Karen and Joshua and asked, "Why do you two hang around with this kid?"

Then Davy turned to Annie. "Hey, as long as you're here, wanna go to the prom with me?"

"NO, you can't take my wife to the prom, either! What makes you think that you can even ask?"

Davy shrugged. "Because you won't let me take your daughter?"

"No son of mine is going to take my daughter OR my wife to—" Carl lapsed into silence when he realized what he was saying. He looked at Annie and sighed, "He did it again, didn't he?"

"I'm afraid so."

"In that case, I'm going to take some aspirin and go to bed," he replied as he left the room.

"Save some aspirin for me, honey," called Annie after him as she followed him.

"Nice going, Batman," said Karen as she patted Davy on the head. "Two more strikes against you."

"Maybe you should just admit defeat.. You don't have many options left," added Joshua.

"HA!" cried Davy as he jumped up out of his chair. "ME? Lose to Omar? NEVER! It's not over yet! I WILL get a prom date!"

* * *

"Dear, would you bring the salad to the table?"

"Sure, Mom," replied Joshua as he went back to the kitchen. "Dad, did you want anything while I'm at it?"

"No, I'm all set, thanks," said his father.

Joshua quickly returned with the salad and placed it on the table before sitting down. Joshua's father asked, "How was your day?"

Just as Joshua was about to reply, the kitchen door burst open. "That stupid Omar, I'll show him!" shouted Davy as he stormed into Joshua's house.

Joshua's parents looked up in surprise as Davy pulled a chair up to the table and began to help himself to dinner. Joshua, on the other hand, casually glanced over and asked, "Why, what happened?"

"Well, I asked that airhead Caitlyn if she would go to the prom, and she spilled the beans," he replied as he stuffed a biscuit in his mouth.

"What beans?"

"She said she wouldn't go with me if I was the last guy in school, and neither would any other girls because Omar told everyone to turn me down," Davy fumed as he stuffed his face.

Joshua thought about this for a moment. "So he put in the fix for you."

"Yeah!" exclaimed Davy, spilling his food across the table. "But I'll fix his little red wagon REAL good! I'll call Immigration and have his student visa revoked and get him deported! That's what I'll do! He isn't as smart as he thinks he is now that I'm on to him!"

Davy reached across the table and grabbed Joshua's glass of milk. "Some people sure have a lot of nerve!" he grumbled as he chugged it down.

"Thanks for the grub, Bub, gotta run again! And remember: I WILL get a prom date!" And with that, Davy charged out the door, leaving Joshua's parents in a state of shock and a swath of destruction at the dinner table to boot.

Joshua just shrugged and plucked a cherry tomato from the mess. "Well, that was my day, Dad. How was yours?"

# Prom Date

# 4

"Here, Buckwheat, take this," said Davy as he held out the spool of wire through the cellar window.

Joshua knelt down to take the spool. "Now what?"

Davy responded to this with his usual crashing and banging around as he made his way around the cellar. "Mom and Dad have too much crap down here," he hollered back. "Just give me a few minutes, okay?"

Joshua stood there holding the spool, wondering what Davy was up to this time. He didn't have to wait long. Davy soon came bounding down the front steps, letting the door slam shut behind him. He hustled over to Joshua and took the spool. "Ok, now hold on to the wire and keep it slack on your end while I unreel the rest of it."

Joshua watched as Davy ran with the wire out into the driveway, cussing as he came to the end of the reel. He stood there for a moment, thinking, then dropped the wire and ran into the garage.

A moment later, Joshua heard the clatter of the tractor as Davy started it up and steered it out to the driveway, parking it next to the end of the wire. Then he hopped off and propped open the battery box while Joshua walked over to see what he was up to.

"So how's the prom date search coming along?"

Davy busied himself pawing through a box of stuff he had brought along as he answered Joshua's question. "Not so good, but I have a plan."

"Is it a good plan?" asked Joshua, although he wasn't sure if he wanted to know.

Davy set about stripping the insulation off the wire and rigging up a switch. "Um, no, not really. Actually, it's a TERRIBLE plan." Then he shrugged his shoulders. "But it's all I have to work with, so it will have to do until I come up with something even worse."

Joshua nodded thoughtfully. "Sort of like the time Cookie Monster beat up Kermit The Frog's rectangle?"

"Mmmm, not quite. It's actually more like when Cookie Monster ate Kermit the Frog's letter W."

Joshua watched as Davy hooked the wires to the terminals. "Speaking of bad plans, what exactly are you doing?"

Davy gave him a quick glance. "I'm hooking up this button to the battery."

"I can see that. Do I want to know why?"

"So I can clean the chimney," replied Davy matter-of-factly.

Joshua looked up at the chimney, then back at Davy. "Ever heard of the law of unintended consequences?"

"Sure I have! But remember, it's not illegal as long as you don't get caught! Wanna push the button?" he asked, holding it out to him.

Joshua shook his head. "No thanks. I'd rather not be an accessory to the crime."

Davy gave him a funny look. "Fine, be that way! But just for that, you have to do the countdown."

Joshua gave a resigned shake of his head. "Ready Batman?  Five...four...three...two...one...ZERO!"

Davy looked up and pushed the button. A short moment later, they watched as a model rocket shot out of the chimney, leaving a trail of black soot behind as it zoomed skyward. There was a moment of silence as the rocket burned the last of its fuel, then exploded in a cloud of snaps and pops.

They watched the remains of the rocket flutter back to earth before Joshua turned to Davy and commented, "I sure hope your plan doesn't backfire like your rocket did."

"Nah, it won't be that spectacular. Remember, I WILL get a prom date!"

# 5

"Ready to go?" asked Joshua, holding out his arm.

Karen gave him a smile and took his arm. "Just about, but we have to wait for Mom to take our picture."

"Again?"

"Mom wants to make sure she gets at least one good shot."

"Speaking of shots, where's your Dad? I thought he'd be the one taking a few shots at me."

"He's a real softy in these moments," answered Annie as she clicked off a few more pictures. "It's a real tear-jerker for him to watch his little girls grow up."

"All set?" asked Karen, changing the subject.

"I think so," answered Annie as she scrolled through the digital format to look at what she had just taken. "That should do be enough. Between yours and Kara's, I have plenty to download and edit. You have a good time and be careful tonight!" she added.

"We will, Mom, thanks!" Karen replied as she and Joshua walked down the driveway. Then Karen looked around. "Hey, where's your car? I didn't even see you pull up in it."

Joshua gave her a mysterious smile. "A funny thing happened to me earlier today."

"Let me guess...the Buckwheat Special fell apart?"

Joshua laughed. "No, not quite. But I did get something special for the occasion," he said as he pointed down the street.

Karen looked at where he was pointing, and her face lit up. "The Corvette? Really? Doesn't that belong to Davy's father?"

"The same one!" he replied as he held the passenger door open for her. "I can't very well take Cinderella to the ball in a pumpkin, can I?"

Karen laughed as she slid down in the seat before

Joshua closed the door and walked around to the other side. As he got in, she commented, "I can't believe you asked him for the Corvette!"

Joshua put on his seatbelt, answering. "Actually, I didn't. He asked me."

"What?"

A puzzled look came over Joshua's face. "It was a funny thing," he explained. "Hiram wanted me to keep it for the weekend while he and Mollie are out of town.  He said he felt better about letting me use it than leaving it in a locked, alarmed garage where Davy could get at it."

With that, Joshua gave the key a quick twist, bringing the Corvette to life before shifting into first and easing out the clutch. Karen didn't say anything for a moment, letting Joshua row through the gears before saying, "Speaking of Davy, did he ever get a prom date?"

Joshua shrugged his shoulders. "I have no idea. I haven't seen or heard from him since school let out yesterday. I haven't been able to reach him, either."

"That's weird. It's not like Davy to vanish like that. You know as well as I do that he isn't going to lose out to Omar."

"Either that or he skipped the country."

Karen thought about this. "Maybe.  But how far is he going to get on twenty dollars?"

# 6

Joshua and Karen were having such a good time at the prom that they nearly forgot about Davy until Omar and his date approached them. "Hey, Joshua! Don't suppose you've seen Davy around this evening, have you?"

Joshua looked a bit surprised. "Why, no, now that you mention it..." He turned to Karen, who shrugged.

"I haven't seen him either, Omar. I thought for sure— hey, look over there!" she said, pointing to the entrance.

Everyone turned to see Davy walking in, dressed in a black tuxedo and with his date on his arm. Omar smiled and shook his head. "I don't believe it! I'll have to give him credit for this one."

"So you lost the bet?" asked Karen.

"Yeah, but it was worth it just to watch him jump through the hoops!" he laughed. Joshua and Karen watched Omar and his date stroll over to Davy and shake his hand before handing the money over.

"Well, I have to hand it to him. I didn't think he'd pull it off," said Karen as Davy came up to them with his date on his arm.

"Hi, Joshua! Hi, Karen! I'd like you to meet Plan B, I mean, Phoebe," he said with great flourish. "Here," he said to her. "Why don't you sit with Karen and get acquainted while Joshua and I get you something to drink?" he asked, pulling a couple of chairs away from a table to seat them. "We'll be right back, okay?"

While Karen and Phoebe were chatting, Davy and Joshua walked over to the refreshment table. "Looks like you did well, Batman. You had me worried for a while! Who is she, anyways?" asked Joshua as he filled some cups with punch.

"Very expensive," replied Davy.

"What?"

"Well," Davy explained. "It's like this. See, first I asked Plan A, but Plan A didn't want to cooperate. We got into a fight about it, and now she's washing chocolate pudding out of her hair... What a rotten sister she is! So then I resorted to Plan B."

"And that is?" asked Joshua.

"I made a fake ID, went to an escort service, and rented Phoebe's company for a couple hours. Tt was all I could afford, so..." He paused when he noticed the look on Joshua's face. "This is one of those times again, isn't it?"

"Yes, Davy, this is definitely one of those times again."

Davy just shrugged. "Oh well, at least I'm only out thirty bucks."

"So you still lost."

"Yeah, but I lost in my favor because I didn't lose to Omar! Besides, she was nice enough to give me a cash discount since Dad won't let me have a credit card and I'm not over twenty-one."

# Prom Date

# 7

Joshua and Karen decided to call it a night; it was getting late, and a number of couples had already left, including Davy and Phoebe.  As they strolled down the hallway to the main entrance, Karen said, "I had a great time tonight!"

"I really enjoyed it, too. It was a lot of fun!" replied Joshua.

Karen gave a happy sigh. "It was nice to meet Phoebe, too. She told me her end of the story. Davy sure got put through the wringer on this one, didn't he?"

Joshua laughed. "He sure did! I wonder if he learned anything from all this?"

"Oh, probably not," she added as Joshua held the door open for her. "Davy wouldn't be Davy if he did."

"Well, I'll go get the car. I have to admit, it's a thrill to be seen in that one. It'll be fun to pick you up in it again! I'll be right back," he said as he walked out into the parking lot, leaving her with several other girls who were also waiting to be seen getting into a limo or expensive car.

It wasn't long before Karen heard a familiar rumble. She turned to see a large shape with one headlight materialize from the darkness. She watched in astonishment as Joshua pulled up in Davy's car and brought it to a creaking halt in front of her.

"Hey, what's this?" she asked. "Where's the Corvette?"

Joshua gave her a silly look as he held out a slip of paper. He took it and read aloud: "You can't get any back seat action in a Corvette! I'll bring it back later tonight. Don't worry, don't stay up, and DON'T tell Dad! XOXOX, Davy."

At this, Karen started to laugh. Joshua started to laugh as well but had to ask, "What?"

"My carriage turned back into a pumpkin!"

Joshua leaped up and bounced across the seat, vaulting himself over the door sill and sweeping Karen off her feet. She shrieked with delight as he spun her around and lifted her over the sill and set her into the seat, adding, "So he put her in a pumpkin shell, and there he kept her very well!"

She gave him a kiss, adding softly, "At least until midnight."

"But it's not midnight yet."

Joshua hustled around to the other side of the car and climbed over the sill and plunked himself behind the wheel. He dropped it into drive, and the engine promptly stalled. Karen began to laugh hysterically as Joshua shoved it back into park, then fumbled with a screwdriver before sticking it into the ignition switch to restart the car.

"Ready to go home?"

"If we make it, Mom has some leftover lasagna in the fridge!"

"That sounds good to me!" agreed Joshua, giving the car a bit of throttle before dropping it into drive. The car hesitated, then lurched forward and away, with the moonlight shining down as Karen snuggled up to Joshua to cap off a perfect evening together.Page Break

# Prom Date

# About The Author

Craig Merrow is a machinist for the United States Navy and enjoys writing, taking courses at the local college, early jazz, old radio shows, picking blueberries, and mountain biking. He is always busy with some new project, his latest being the design and construction of an off-grid solar home in Southern Maine.

# About The Publisher

Story Shares is a nonprofit focused on supporting the millions of teens and adults who struggle with reading by creating a new shelf in the library specifically for them. The ever-growing collection features content that is compelling and culturally relevant for teens and adults, yet still readable at a range of lower reading levels.

Story Shares generates content by engaging deeply with writers, bringing together a community to create this new kind of book. With more intriguing and approachable stories to choose from, the teens and adults who have fallen behind are improving their skills and beginning to discover the joy of reading. For more information, visit storyshares.org.

Easy to Read. Hard to Put Down.